I0536989

Apocalypse Relief

Lula Lucent

Ghost Festival Press

APOCALYPSE RELIEF

Part of the Reprobates™ series, Novella the Second

Published by Ghost Festival Press

Copyright © 2023 by Lula Lucent

Cover art by Les Solot

ISBN: 978-0-9906078-6-1

First edition: August 15, 2023
Duggery Day

Printed on Earth

That which saves and is saved.

Our new reality is excruciating to chronicle; each word written is a monument that will never erode. In my attempt to make sense of much madness, I instead make that madness more real. May our beloved God of All Creation, now dead and soon-to-be forgotten, forgive me for my self-serving compulsion. My inkwell is diluted with shame.

Somewhere it is raining vinegar. Somewhere else a cliffside curdles into fleshy biomass. Somewhere the sky has shattered and through a crack, wide as hatred, pools the blood of murdered stars. Somewhere else the very air is invisible knives, and to breathe it is to serrate the throat and flense the lungs. What can possibly save us?

In the Month of Dust – after faith was lost – the poorest of the poor encountered it, though they did not know that at the time. Such unending torments had been since the passing of the Harbingers that purest compassion had come and gone from their midst, and they scarcely even realized.

From the east, salvation came defying the sunset; upon sturdy backs succor was borne; overflowing hearts beat with empathy; arms extended to all, and in those tender hands: fresh water, nourishing food, bandages, and care.

And then they rejoiced: "Who fed me when I was starving? Who comforted me when I lay in sickness?"

The Healers of the Apocalypse.

Their names and their virtues joined as one:

PEACE

HOPE

CHARITY

LOVE

*Although I am
unworthy of the task
I will now mark
the hours of the struggle.*

May we awaken to our promises.

Apocalypse Relief

The First Sorrow

Into the moors of Inirnith they stride while the land languishes in agony. Here do they resolve to begin their ministry, tending to the impossible task of saving the world. Despite their most holy and noble goal, their true mission – unspoken for fear that it is fragile and would crack from mere utterance – is to find Daeli, to inspire her to return. But none know where she has gone, and I will not say.

They meet no living soul on their march through fields gone bleak, strewn with weeds that choke like nooses the sunflowers now bent to the ground in submission. Not once do their footsteps falter. They have seen worse; they will see worse yet.

A hunched, hulking form kneels in their path, sunk into the peat. At the sound of their procession, it turns its head. Rusted metal screams.

"Poor thing," Hope says, as she rubs grime from its alien features and peculiar face.

The others shake their heads in dismay. There was once a teeming kingdom nestled where they stand, within wild grasslands that spread a bounty of harvests to every horizon. And the only thing left, it now appears, is a mechanical automaton.

"Are we truly too late to offer anyone more than mourning? Has tragedy been sown, and our choice is either to witness or to reap?" Charity asks.

The scarecrow stands with visible effort. Its gears whine and moan.

"Perhaps our metal friend can guide us," Love says.

It gazes down upon the four humans it towers over, nothing of emotion in its gaze nor in its halting movements. It simply exists and does not understand the purpose of a life that has failed in its directive. The fields are gone.

"Yes," Peace speaks at last, "let this strange creature show us the way. Pray, let it bring us to the wounded and the lost."

And so it does. The broken scarecrow brings them to other scarecrows: most dead and insensate; some perhaps recoverable; others, beyond reason, who plant pebbles under inert soil, waiting for a growth that will never come, while their sickles rust uselessly at their sides.

But those that can move travel with them, until there are dozens, and after surveying the destruction of nature they come upon the castle town that is now a tomb.

The gates are barred from within, but that which is old and rotten cannot withstand the blows of the scarecrows; once proud woodwork is reduced to splinters. Warily do the Healers proceed down streets pulsing with unnatural silence. I have not described, nor will I ever, the slaughter they beheld other than to write this:

They wept.

And after weeping, they went to work. From home to home, courtyard to courtyard, down in the humblest corner of the lowliest pauper's shack to the highest spire of the empress's retreat in the lofty castle above, they treated each corpse they found with special ointments, foreign herbs, and devout prayers.

Sunlight and wind have always been blessings bestowed upon Inirnith. And so the Healers – though they could not carry every body – ensured that light could enter every window, and wind could enter every doorway, until the overwhelming stench of death and decay was carried away. Only a delicate scent not unlike lilies remained.

The four part from one another, hurrying to every church to gather what little consecrated water has not yet dried in the basins of their sacristies. They rejoin in the belfry of the abbey where carillons once rang with praises to God's glory and celebrations of heavenly joy.

Above the stark silence of cold Inirith, the Healers recite an elegy to lay the dead to rest, and sprinkle sacral water into the stirring wind to spare their bodies from rot.

The first sorrow is healed.

> Rejoice as I do.
> There will be more.
> This renewal is one that comforts.

And so preservation begins:

Funerals for the dead
bound together in sighs
on a tree of living release.
Pious remembrance of a time
now   passed,   passing   on
the enduring price: absence godly.
Grass   withers,   springs   forth
promised   days   growing   cold,
sun   dimly   glowing   in   defeat.
Dandelion   tears   taking   flight
and   then   so   calmly   nigh
holy   ground   hallowed   by   peat.
Whispered   words   to   the   gloom,
new   friendship   will   bloom,
my   peace   undisturbed
when   the   dawn   breaks.

Before the Healers leave, they teach the scarecrows how to perform burials. There will come a time much later when others will aid in this burden, and many hands will make the load lighter. But who can say if the scarecrows truly understand that, in this task, there will be no harvest?

It may be that their fate is to wait forevermore in vain. And yet, though we do not know and cannot know, perhaps they instead stand vigil for something we cannot imagine. In years yet to come, or in centuries past measure, it may well be that flowers here will grow. And even if all the Earth lies barren, these manufactured men will tend tiny petals with the dew that glistens each morning upon their greaves.

Apocalypse Relief

The Second Sorrow

Quiet tragedies await the Healers wherever they go. There are no end to them. Survivors are scattered; resources meagre; the light of the sun is fading fast, more each passing day. An eternal nightfall settles in with the permanence of the grave. What new evils will that final day usher forth? The prophecies do not say.

Goodness is left in their wake. And a single person can accomplish much in life; four can do so much more. They direct the survivors to safety; they find new sources of food; they kindle a little light inside darkened hearts and, in time, this may be enough.

Even a cinder can transcend inferno.

Along the edges of poisoned Willow Way, the Healers come upon the remnants of Daeli's Crusade. Their tents are in poor condition, ripped and muddied, and the breeze that flutters by makes the canvas look like dried human skins. The troops are haggard from eating forest fauna no longer fit for consumption.

"What else can be done?" they moan aloud. "God is dead, and likely Daeli – and we have betrayed them both."

It is difficult to pity those who cause their own downfall, who chose unkindness towards one who was only ever kind. When we ask the seers "What is the greatest of sins?" the answer we receive is: "Suicide of the body." But is denying a second chance to any who repent not the worst of these? It becomes a suicide of the spirit and denies redemption.

"Seek you any yet living," Hope tells them. "Go forth. Find them. Defend them from what wickedness you can. And if you cannot, and have also lost the swords in your hearts, go forth and do harm no more."

And a murmur went through those assembled, and like a languid stream they flowed away from the rotting woods, leaving their tents behind. Once all had gone, a solid silence attached itself to the Healers and followed them past the threshold of trees.

Willow Way is weeping. Noxious fumes seep from the very ground. With cloaks drawn tight as makeshift masks, the Healers creep about and tarry nowhere. Such is the perversion of the forest that the despair the fallen crusaders gave voice to was not without reason.

Peace studies a skinny branch, hanging from a thread of gray tendon from the bloated trunk of what was once an oak. The lightest brush of his finger tears it from the bole, causing the roots around his feet to spasm in agony.

"This is beyond my skills," Peace admits.

"Beyond us all," Love mourns.

And yet Charity and Hope refuse to agree. They approach the native wildlife – terrified and dangerous as each creature has become – and touch them tenderly, offer gentle words and whispers full of promises of soothing. Those that do not flee, or attack, tremble in piteous fear at the chanting of healing incantations.

Wounds heal in seconds. Vigor returns. Rage subsides. And though a fear remains, and with it confusion, the animals regain their senses and a second chance at life.

Charity watches as each healed creature bounds away for the treeline to escape this blighted land. "Is it enough?"

The silence stirs.

"Brave humans," croaks a twisted voice, "it is."

Now turning to behold the speaker, all saw that same silence that had been stalking them reveal itself. In form it was lithe and, while resembling a woman, had horny growths upon the crown of its head. One arm was missing at the elbow, and it stood with difficulty on knees that bent inwards at unnatural angles. But its face was serene, as though earthly pains were but memories and its destroyed body no more substantial.

Love rushes forward, a spell of fortitude on his lips. But the creature merely smiles wider, dissuading the impulse. "My soma is gone. I am not as I was. No magick can help."

And thus does Laurelai return to this tale, something lesser yet on the verge of becoming so much greater than ever before. For now, she is their guide in a forest as broken as she. The trails by which she leads are full of perils, but the Healers are no strangers to these times. Nowhere is safe.

They ask after her quest and are amazed to learn that she too seeks Daeli in her own way. She tells them of the confrontation with the Harbingers, how the Lightbringer stood alone against pure evil, and was defeated before battle could be joined. Despite this, truest Laurelai had sought to speak with her, to join her just cause even after it had been scorned and abandoned by her staunchest allies.

"But Daeli, blessed of God, walked away. For a time, she waited... for something that did not come, it seemed. Though I was!" Laurelai cries with pride. "I was coming to her side, where I belong, but my gait was halting and I fell often, and when I was nearly upon her: she walked away, and I could not follow."

And the Healers said in turn, "We too know not where she has gone, nor what has taken her from us."

Then they spoke of their own mission, finding strength in Laurelai's conviction to finally voice it aloud. And once they had spoken, they found that their dream was not fragile, nor the words that voiced it, and the gloom of the woods lessened, and the dappled light – though scant – penetrated the smothering canopy overhead and caused the strange eyes of their friend to sparkle and flare bright as emeralds.

The hand of God of All Creation, this humble chronicler notes, moves in mysterious ways even after having ceased to move at all. For though It had been removed from existence, Its movements lingered on like a wind that no longer has an origin yet a tremendous speed that can never fully stop.

"But why do you now seek her?" asks Charity.

"I will be the dawn," says Laurelai, gazing skywards. "Daeli Lightbringer will be what comes after."

So the companions continue forward, emboldened by their common cause in a forest that, though dying, is not yet dead. All plant life, if it can be called such, has been so corrupted that it scarcely resembles its original form, and is therefore even more dangerous. There are some hollows that even Laurelai refuses to enter. When she nears one of these spaces of total corruption, she bids them halt, approaches the nearest tree, and presses her face against the trunk. Then its bark shimmers like disturbed water, and she plunges her head into its interior. Truly, the faefolk are queer indeed.

"The way is closed," she will say, and lead them elsewhere. Or at times, "This way will permit us," and lead them on.

In the furthest depths where the ground has collapsed into barrows now desecrated, a horrible cave gapes. This is where the Harbingers extirpated the heart of the only home that Laurelai has ever known. She will never ask if that event could have been prevented had she become, as the elder faefolk assumed, the ruler of them all. No. She lives only in the sunlight and in a future her faith is revealing daily.

The Healers approach this void. Perhaps if they venture inside, they can heal Willow Way. And Daeli, wherever she may be, whatever she may be feeling, would notice this change and behold poisonous fumes dispersing upon sweet winds. Would that call her back? O Daeli!

For now, they are beset by so many wretched things: blood maggots, cyst-spiders, root phasmids, fungal fetches. Peace and Love, inspired by the small victories that Charity and Hope had won, chant their restorative magicks. But this cannot come to good, for none of these foul abortions of creation have an original form in which to return. Every one was birthed by the dread power of the Harbingers who knew nothing of teaching offspring and left them all in ignorance. And so, to survive, the Healers brandish their staves and, unbowed, carpet the ground with monstrous blood.

It should be noted, and here in the early pages it must, that this is the pacificism of the wilderness: wishing harmony unto all things, but when threatened with unsought violence to echo that harm back with such atavistic force that the aggressor is eradicated, and silence reigns. In such a manner did Laurelai fall upon these things in spite of her disabilities. Astonished by the sight, the hearts of the Healers were roused and they crushed bones to dust and slew anything that spewed forth from the blackness.

The battle quietens. There is a stillness. They wonder if another attack is imminent, or if it is over. Peace creeps to the edge of the gaping pit and thrusts within a magick torch. The very shadows scream in terror, each one composed of hundreds of mouths and each mouth filled with hundreds of fangs. The four retreat, clutching their ears; Laurelai stands motionless, green ichor dribbling from her horns.

"We must descend," they say.

"Then descend you will," quoth Laurelai, weaving of her leafy hair a charm to dull their senses. "Know that you will know deafness, and so all of your eyes must be as ears as one to another."

Hope quavers. "Then, will you leave us?"

"Beyond that gate, powerlessness lies," she proclaims, "For I am of Willow Way, and that within is Willow Way undone." At this she raises her severed arm. "I can alter the course of the poison that courses through me, and I can unbreak my broken body by making sacrifices of other parts, but to enter therein is to cease to be Laurelai and become someone else. I can not allow this."

The Healers accept the bracelets their protectress offers, and one by one enter the barrows. If the flicker of a single torch frightened the shadows, the brilliance of four instills in them a feeling of doom so profound that the wails they emit can be heard as far away as Kharhoom. But to these bold women and men, there is naught but blessed silence.

This serenity, however, does not extend to their sight. What horrors they behold! Generations upon generations of corpses interred in the barrows, partially-digested by the dirt, spasm as in the throes of endless orgasms, spurting out entrails from wherever they have rotted holes.

Bones are everywhere and powder underfoot. Each step is a desecration. It is impossible to proceed with hallowed respect. None of the healers, neither Love nor Peace nor Hope nor Charity, are without tears. Though more polluted monsters will harry their descent, and even now creep from the shadow-mouths behind their backs, they are unable to escape the shame of violating this already profaned boneyard.

What purity! How can I not be moved, as they, when I recall their burdens? And what righteous fury falls upon the skulking monsters when they, in rank foolishness, spring out with expectation of easy prey. For it is not force of arms or thought or sinew that powers the downward strokes of each staff. No! It is outrage! It is revulsion! It is divine fire, that which constricts the hearts of all good mortal kin on Earth – when they witness such wrongs as these – and then erupts in holy immolation. There are no words to adequately describe such a feeling as theirs but to say this: though darkness may hide in places where there is light – yea, though it may dwell in the cathedral of the soul itself – there is, and always will remain, a searing brightness in the human heart from which no shadow may ever hide.

What a lamentation there would have been if only evil could mourn. If any had lived through that moment when the Healers felt no tears of mercy for the foul things worming in the bowels of the dirt, the end might have come more swiftly and more gently. Instead, the howls that poured out of the maw of that cave caused all things to tremble save one. And that was Laurelai, who trembled in reverie, whose poisoned veins seared with an epiphany that would stir a turning of the world.

The second sorrow is healed.

Rejoice as I do.
There will be more.
This renewal is one that breathes.

And so restoration begins:

> *Lichens clinging to rock*
> *refuse   to   relent*
> *in   an   embrace*
> *of   a   dusty   decision   now   forgot.*
> *The   old   world   moves*
> *not   for   days*
> *but   for   ages   unnamed*
> *uncounted   by   ivy   drawn   taut.*
> *The   flow   of   time   is   reconsidered*
> *hours   minutes   seconds: not   enough.*
> *Dividing   instants   into   specks   of   earth*
> *until   nothing   is   sloughed.*
> *Wood remembers the green, leaf recalls the moisture,*
> *soil   saturates   with   flooding   memories,*
> *roots   as   united   as   my   veins   spreading   wide*
> *interconnected reliquaries.*

The pall of contagion that blanketed so heavily upon the vastness of Willow Way lifts, a phantasm fleeing before the break of day, and floats heavenwards until – diluted and stretched thin as ribbons – it is gone.

But that is all. The rhizome of the forest runs deep, and the harm of the Harbingers deeper still. There is only so much humanity can do. It has been seen, and will be seen again, that this has ever been so. For the trees themselves remain sickly and half-dead.

It seems to the Healers, victory fading fast, that the need for Daeli is all the more urgent, and they vow to kindle light until her downcast eyes glimpse a flicker of her own.

Apocalypse Relief

The Third Sorrow

Rumors whisper. Thoughts disquiet. More forces are at work than those herein inscribed, as ephemeral as speech yet equally potent. There are truths. There are lies. But when God of All Creation was slain, the gap between that which is and that which is not bridged. And some lies became truths. Rumors multiplied. Thoughts solidified. With them came the Doomsayer.

It is said that he walks endlessly, never tiring, slowing for no thing, and if you spy him from afar even at the sunrise he is walking, and if you spy him from afar even at the sunset, he is still walking. And whither does he go? From town to town, city to city, kingdom to kingdom, proclaiming that doom is come.

None have seen him and yet all swear to have heard of his comings and goings from the mouths of others. At times these stories fade into the corners of dreams, a restlessness of the mind that cannot describe what disturbs its stillness. But then there are the settlements that lay in the interstitial places in between, neither fully on the plains or by the forest or in the desert, that frenzy.

The Healers find emptiness there. Within each home: supper uneaten, chairs thrown to the floor, a memory of panic trapped frozen in time. Every scene is slightly different, but some details are fixed as if nailed to the very atmosphere: footprints missing from the ground; a silence that throbs to agony the more it is focused upon; an acrid scent wafting of butchered offal, charcoal, and petrichor. Whenever they follow this reek, they discover a single pebble cowering in the dirt. It is rounded by pockmarked ridges; when lifted and set within the palm of a hand, it is heavy as an iron ingot. It trembles briefly, then is still.

They always bury it, and speak of it no more.

Words are now laden with other substances, intent and meaning mere idle passengers. The Healers fear speaking for anything said wrongly may ill creation form.

They witness Glassmere and can do nothing. Weeping is denied them, and catharsis another word drained of worth until it is fragile, translucent skin. Mount Ordeal has already begun to crack under its own weight; all they can do is watch the dust settle, and walk on. By the time I finish this page, it will have shattered again; when I, at last, set down the pen, there will be nothing left to buckle.

For long stretches of time, they trek towards a hint of smoke over a mirage-bright horizon that cannot be reached. Never nearing, they quail. Trodden discolored miles beneath their heels shift from drab rock to burnt grass to solid metal. Laurelai, lost in reverie, plants her feet upon a whorl of brass and silver, and raises her hand at the dimming sun.

Abide in my roots
O Wondrous Light
the warmth of noon
throughout dark night.

Stir my leaves
O Wind of Dawn
reminding heartwood
of eternal song.

Her words comfort. And Peace, heartened, turns his shared thought into a charge of faith: "We will not give up."

To speak this on the border of what was once Kharhoom is bold indeed. It is ever a trifle to steel oneself in the shade of a tree, or fireside by a hearth, but to say it aloud during this time – when some truths can become lies – and at this place – where now and here conjoin into a vasty nowhere – risks sabotaging their great work before it has barely begun. Yet although none knew then, and may not now, these words might have secured them future victories. For if evil so inclined can bridge the gap between realities, so can good.

Each Healer must hold firm to their belief from this exact moment until the end. Paralyzed Kharhoom is a more hostile region than ever it was when filled with sand and desolation. Sunlight reflects off polished surfaces, an ocean of metallic crests and troughs, that magnify any light to piercing blindness and oppressive heat. The smooth ground too is hazardous, causing them to slip and fall and bruise their knees and hands as they stumble without sight. When Hope sobs after enduring a particularly egregious impact, Laurelai bids them halt.

"I must tarry a while," says she. "Beyond Willow Way, nourishment I draw from the day. By night, no longer have I will as thee. Friends, gather around."

And at this, she broke off branches from her crippled arm and plucked roots from her stomach, and fashioned for each Healer a mesh for their weary soles that would grip into the surface of the melted desert.

"Will you be safe without us?" Charity asks.

"Worry not for me," says Laurelai. "This is not where my ending will bloom."

In darkness, the Healers find solace to go on. Warmed in spirit by the kindness of their strange companion, and in body by the radiating glow of the metallic ground, they continue forward with as much vim as after a good sleep. They follow echoes, seeking survivors, but find only themselves as the cause of each new disturbance: Hope's timid greeting to a shadow passing overhead returned one hour later, devoid of her emotion and as though the syllables had been soaked in acid; when Peace clapped his hands, in genuine mirth at a fond memory, frightening thunderclaps returned; and when Love led vespers, all singing a favored hymnal, the reverence of that liturgy was abruptly forgotten when raving squeals and death wails descended upon them at compline until they clutched at each other, crying as quietly as they could for fear of how their sobs might return.

That midnight, they observed a greater silence. Yet, needing company, they gathered close to one another and whispered in the gloom.

"Has our journey gone awry of purpose?" Charity asked. "Inhospitable the desert always was. And so, waste we time stalking mirages when so many need us elsewhere?"

"The smoke," Love reminded her.

"Even I have wondered…" Hope murmured in doubt.

Peace closed his eyes. "Who else, but we, would look?"

At length they debated what felt, in the middle of the night, a fool's errand. And it is good that they did so, for above their heads mist wraiths were soaring and weaving their sorceries to snare darkling energy that invisibly budded out of the anguish in the air, like dew upon grass. Neither these predators nor their prey have existed on our plane since the age of the Fallen. Has the wreckage wrought by the Harbingers brought these forth from extinction? Or has time now become a fickle thing, making antiquity live again?

But a fight they were ill-equipped to endure did not occur that night. The rustle of the wraiths and the whispering of the Healers was to be a passing in the dark: shadows bound for other horizons.

False dawn ushers them the question of their purpose, and they answer with footsteps aimed towards the center of Kharhoom. Soon, the smoke reappears. Soon, they hasten their steps. Soon, there is music. Soon, they nearly run. Soon, the sooty mirage is what it was: murders upon murders of crows, circling without end.

Do you know what they circle? I will tell you what your heart already mourns: Cloud Kingdom, crucified to the sky; Nimbus, weeping for its ruin in the quiet pattering of rain. The Healers are blessed with ignorance; they have no conception of the tragedy that was, is, will be. Instead, like children, they scurry around in the shade, seeking for a thing that is far above their reach if ever their eyes had seen.

The hateful nail the Harbingers used to climb is broken. There can be no more ascension here. And if there could, what would possibly be the result? Any corpses that remain could neither be recovered nor interred. And any living that remain could neither be healed nor consoled. Some things are beyond mortal ken.

Yet recall that some impossible things may now be. For in some ways I describe from habit a world that is no longer, rather than the realm of possibility we find ourselves within. So I will tell this next part plain and stark that all may be awed by its simple truth.

The demons came for them.

Burning from the sun, flaring from the reflecting metal, the first wave of demons came running and yammering. Weapons raised, with no memories of the peaceful millennia beneath Ordeal, with lust for war and blood alone.

And the Healers led them, as though sidestepping for an unruly mutt, into the sprinkling rains. The demons doused, one by one, fires quenched despite the sun, despite the heat, one by one returning to their senses in an instant, memories flooding back of the bedrock tunnels and architectural achievements and the smithies ringing with hammers like church bells at lauds, and one by one they held each other, keening for the loss of their hard-won innocence that the Harbingers had so unknowingly raped from them.

The second wave halted in their militant tracks, clashed their weapons against the ground, and mindlessly sought a way to bring the Healers from their protective curtain wall. But cleverness can come from the most unlikely miens. Peace extended a hand beyond the rain, darting away from the stroke of a hammer, using that momentum to trip demons again and again. Each fell into a puddle, stared for a time bewildered at the clouds above, and blinked away raindrops commingled with tears.

Thusly, the battle that never was ended.

One among the demonic horde, whose name it would be disrespectful to note per the dictates of their culture, bows low before the Healers and humbly asks parley.

"This cannot be so, for you and I are not at war," Peace gently declines.

The demon bows lower, near enough to the ground, and a murmur rumbles through the horde. Here is a human who can stand against a tide and turn it with grace and humility. But the crowd did speak there beneath the rain and when the final word had been spoken, the demons were aggrieved to learn of the ease with which evil had upended the sanctity and the durable foundations of the Earth.

"One day will the sun wink out and eternal night descend," the demon proclaims. "Long have we longed for such a thing, so that we might rebehold the surface of the Old World once more. I have only read in the aged tablets of the beauty of thy homelands, dearest humans. But I would that we had stayed underground forever than a single blade of thy grass had been marred underhoof by those defilers. This cannot come to any good."

"But good has come, for lo!" cries Love aloud. "Sunlight illumes your bodies, and you are not aflame."

And so it is: an impossibility shining beneath the rubble of a derelict kingdom in the heavens, an empty home bereft of angels and music and song, eternally raining holy water that has blessings yet.

The Healers are divinely inspired by the realization and lead the demons in dance, circling without end in opposition to the gyre of crows, with jubilation that is too profound for words.

A raised arm to say: "Thank you."
A bow to say: "You're welcome."
A pirouette to say: "Come with me."
A stride to say: "I will follow."
A pause to say: "Amen."

The third sorrow is healed.

Rejoice as I do.
There will be more.
This renewal is one that soothes.
And so purification begins:

*Caressing   beams
so   quietly   stream
have   no   need   for   words   anymore.
What   has   been   thought
has   been   said   and   has   brought
finality   to   intentions   of   yore.
Harsh   colors   drain   away
pastel   shadows   betrayed
the   lustre   of   a   breeze   that   refracts.
Dominion   prolonged   settles
in   for   a   sleep
ancient   and   demoniac.
How   deep   is   the   sigh
that   eases   the   sky
holding   my   breath
in   sanctity.*

Snow is falling. The crows disperse to the corners of the world; they have become pure white. Gray clouds vivify into an eternal vision of spring. Even the spike that pierces from the ground is bleached as if in shame.

Is this miracle? No. Not yet. It is still too soon for those. This is something else. Something new. Something sublime. The Healers soak bandages in holy water pools, make poultices, fill waterskins. And the demons coat themselves in holy snow, horns and all, and with voices that could only come from the secret pockets of the deep, they wield their tools for their true purposes and burrow into the ground. Metal crumbles like dirt, and soon tunnels spirit them away.

Apocalypse Relief

The Fourth Sorrow

There are those who have begun to see the signs left for Daeli. Corpses upon the plains buried by gentle scarecrows; misty poisons no longer permeating the forest canopies; ubiquitous white crows singing songs filled with undiluted release. Like catching sight of the first buds of spring after a terrible winter, hearts are stirring to the vision of the promise of a real tomorrow, and imagined tomorrows beyond.

Yet chaos provides opportunities for both good and evil. For there are some eyes that have seen these signs and hastened their wickedness. Even now, they seek to purge this progress and rip it squalling from the womb.

Within the ground, all is silent. The Healers are waiting, their demonic allies listening. It is not long before rumbling again crosses overhead. They are too far below the surface to know what it is, but it sounds like a malevolent army on the march. But whose forces can it be? Surely new powers have not yet arisen from the ashes of cataclysm.

Someone is searching for them.

And when all is silence again, the demons continue to burrow onwards. It was they that first suggested digging upwards to scout, to meet this unknown foe as necessary, but counsel said the risk of losing their senses was too great and the holy snow that coated them too dear a boon to sacrifice; Peace had noted it would preserve indefinitely in the coolness of the caverns. And so delve they did into earthly darkness and away from the noises of the overworld.

Colossal chambers they discover at the farthest ends of their tunnels, glittering with star-like jewels and gemstones covering the walls like fogbanks, all amber of dawn and violet of dusk. A single drop of water echoes. The tranquility is sacred relief after leagues of constant digging.

They sleep, eat, revise maps made of interchangeable precious stones that are more meaningful to demons than family trees are to humankind. For each map is shared history and covenant with their grandsires to live on.

Millennia have the demonic horde lived beneath both ground and notice of the sunlit world. It is true that many, even the wisest, had forgotten of their existence or had come to misbelieve they and the Fallen angelic choir had fought to mutual annihilation. Thus, the demons were wholly ignorant of the events that propelled them into feral frenzy and the resulting tragedies – as have been chronicled.

The Healers take turns in the telling of the tale of the Harbingers, of the ruin they brought forth from their prison in Hell, and the consequences to the Earth, the Divine, and every thing in between.

It is a solemn storytelling.

And when it is concluded they burrow onward, speaking no words. They have much to think on, home is distant yet, and the abiding shadows have much to remind them.

Far away and far above, Laurelai in solitude proceeds. She is rested and recovered from dormancy, and takes a careful step at a time. Her gifts to the Healers have cost her dearly: there is less of her, and more of poison, every day. When she walks, she walks as if with a palsy and the going is painstaking, though thankfully without pain.

Does she follow Love, and Charity, and Peace, and Hope? I do not know. The daughter of Willow Way has ever gone wherever the wind wills; even now, slowly and haltingly, she is singing with her own voice, she is dancing with her own feet, she is living through her body and becoming one with that which still exists upon the other side.

Blessed is Laurelai among all creatures, proud or meek, for life does not diminish the song in her heart. Yea, though the beat of its mysterious rhythms is as unknowing as it is unknowable, she changes her breathing and shifts her stance, and always Laurelai remains.

One day she will be called Truest Friend, as never there has been before. But until such time, let all let her be as she is in this moment: alive and free and herself.

When she reaches the edge of the prairie, the gray throng is already there – that fell force which is seeking the Healers. It passes before her. She continues on. It passes behind her. She continues on. Day and night, without pause, they both move with purposes of their own. The throng crisscrosses the ashen grasslands, nearly discovering Laurelai with every crossing, and yet they do not, and do not know of her passage, and not once has she faltered, and not once has she been afeared, and she is fully aware of their passage.

One morning they are simply gone, and Laurelai does not wonder after them. She stops before tattered banners, vaguely the color of saffron after so much time bleached by the sun, and is greeted by rusty swords and splintery shields and the kind of faces that pariahs know very well.

"Is Daeli among you?" she asks the Broken Crusade.

Swords and shields lower in shame for the second time in this world, yet now for a new reason and this time they are neither dropped nor thrown away.

"Our leader is not," answers the old man with half-blind eyes. "Though were it so, we would be unworthy of hosting the Lightbringer."

"I am seeking her," Laurelai explains, "and soon must find her. To whom do I speak?"

"My lady, you address no one," he says, "as we are unworthy of our names – as we are unworthy of speaking the name of the Lightbringer. Therefore we have sworn an oath to deny ourselves all comforts, to march throughout the land with these banners we once scorned, until we have helped every being our cruelties have harmed, and their forgiveness earned."

What he leaves unspoken are the souls already departed who can never be helped and whose forgiveness can never be earned. Such is the tribulation of life: that choices made in lusty passions can so coldly usher forth days bleak and griefs unassuaged.

And thus hoisting the faded banners upon their bruised shoulders, the Broken Crusade continues towards the barren horizon amidst the receding rays of sun. Laurelai moves on, joyfully singing ever.

In their chests, the demonic horde has begun to feel a stirring akin to this music as they near the outskirts of their subterranean citadels. The final mile of bedrock is the most difficult to bore through, not from its thickness but the unknown mystery beyond. They are frightened to gaze upon, eyes unclouded, the destruction of that which is bastion.

When they crack the outermost layer, every demon flinches away and covers their eyes. The Healers stand in amazement, beckoning the wisps of light that have illuminated the excavation, then walk into umbral shadow. But darkness does not persist, for their sight adjusts erelong to sunbeams streaming from a riot of angles through the ceiling of the cavern as if penetrated by thousands of consecrated spears. And indeed they may as well have been: the demons shiver, refuse to enter in, knowing that if a single thread of light touches them, they could ignite once more to blazing and warmongering.

"Be of good cheer; the snow protects," comforts Hope.

"We dare not take such risk," the eldest demon moans. "In a single second lost we centuries of heedful progress. If it be safe, as thou claim, we must beg thy forbearance."

"Friends, we will go ahead of them," Peace suggests. "Think on how we felt to observe the lands of our birth collapsing and festering, the unrelenting deathwatch that was each passing minute. Come. Let us be their eyes that they may later be our hands."

What a ruinous sight greets them all. The proud towers surrounding Pinnacle Keep buried in forced humility; the Aqueduct Argent, that served as river transport for an age, spewing forth clotted scum on the settlements far below; Manse Cathedral reduced to sacrilegious debris.

A shrieking bursts from the domed firmament, and rocks clatter, settle, then go quiet. The hollowed mountains repose in their irregular descent: Ordeal's slow assisted suicide.

"What can our slight powers avail us in such catastrophe as this? Here are no survivors. We have helped those we could. Stand we vigil? Sing services for the forgotten? What ministry can we offer more than pity?" they ask.

And yet they meander the sundered streets not knowing what they seek, with feet seemingly knowing exactly where they are going. Perhaps it is their familiarity with devastation that tugs their hearts in the right direction before their minds are focused fully. Charity discovers an uncracked jar with silvery-white liquid sloshing inside; Hope unearths pottery etched with jocular scenes; Peace unhooks a dusty tome from copper chains binding it to a bookcase of steel; and Love unfurls a tapestry ornately embroidered depicting the entirety of the world, including those expanses the four had never known existed.

"How delightful it all feels when stitched so small!" Love exclaims, forgetting at once the despair that had afflicted their hearts.

"I confess I must apologize to the demonsire when next we meet," Peace admits, carefully shutting the pages of the book, "as this appears to be a personal journal, though I cannot read the words."

"This too has more narrative than I at first expected!" Hope declares, marveling at figures of demons and angels upon the pot within her hands.

But Charity could only smile to herself, giggle under a sweetened breath, and take another sip from the contents of the jar. She had found a liquor that was most potent indeed.

Despite the innumerable dangers, they explore and find many more an item of worth, and much of demonic industry yet unscathed by the downfall of the earth. Though there is catastrophe here, it has not enveloped everything in full.

And then they relate these discoveries to the demons, some of whom are bold enough to risk the beams of light, and all of whom are reinvigorated to know their precious history has not been utterly expunged.

The eldest demon explains that what the Healers carry are four relics dating to the foundation of the Underworld. Charity, it must be noted, is duly embarrassed for sampling a taste of the past, and wisely keeps her peace if not her temperance.

When gloaming comes, the demons hurry to save what can be saved. The mountains above tremble; night presses down with such unnatural force that cracks spread across the breadth of the dome like a swarm of skittering spiders end-to-end. The Healers go separate ways, each leading an excavation team. With illuming magicks they light the way around perilous pitfalls; with strengthening enchantments they bolster buildings just prior to their collapse, allowing precious contents to be carried out and away; and with sincere compassion they instill in the demons an inner peace as they wend through the avenues of sobering waste.

Only those of us who have lost can know such pains as they and the value of those things that, when collected together, make a home.

And the instant the four groups converge at the entrance to the cavern with celebrations in their minds, they witness in dismay each and every object – so carefully carried away – disintegrating into piles of rust. Without caution for whatever could be causing this deterioration, the Healers cry out in alarm for the demons to disperse. Chanting and holding aloft their staves, they lay a blessing upon ancient works of art, treasures both precious and personal, and far too many heirlooms of the countless dead who fell in war with the angels before they knew transcendent calm.

Some trace of divinity must have heard, in Its passing, their words. For those salvaged things were preserved.

The fourth sorrow is healed.

Rejoice as I do.

There will be more.

This renewal is one that endures.

And so reformation begins:

Holocaust drowned
wildfire deluged
bonfire drenched
in trebled redemption, anew.
History cannot wash
away the stains of sin,
but flesh may be cleansed
and robes dyed in whites.
A face of wrinkles, lined
and written in foreign words:
the ink must never dry.
Another chance.   Another chance.
Brick ruptures.   Stone fissures.
Yet mortar is the binding of the hands
holding hands holding hands while
yesterday exalts tomorrow with my tears.

In newer tunnels, in lower pits, the demons cook a feast. Furnace smoke pours out of burrows to the overground, and some reaches their old abandoned citadels miles away, wafting upward until it steams through the holes in Ordeal. Later, smoke from implements of industry will issue forth an announcement that they are returned.

Peace, Love, Hope, and Charity are honored guests at this table of demons who will remain safe here even when the mountain has finally sunk into the plains. But such safety and quietude are not fated for these four. Newly provisioned, they can only rest their heels but briefly.

The dying world awaits.

Apocalypse Relief

The Fifth Sorrow

The time of gentle victories is over. If there is to be any further goodness won, it will now come at a cost so high that we will question if the effort was worth such commitment. But the Healers of the Apocalypse are not aware of this fact – or if they are, they have resolved to see this through come what may.

And it will. There is no stopping it.

Towards the outlet of subterranean tunnels, they perhaps at least sense this futility. Passing within old demon caves, now frozen solid, they see a gray writhing mass through the ice overhead. The crevasses are increasingly difficult to squeeze between, and so they are forced to listen to its labor. Many miles away they emerge into the outer reaches, still hearing muffled screaming which has not once abated for breath. The echo will live permanently in their memories.

Though at the time there was no name for the place they found themselves within, today we begrudgingly know it as the Graveyard of All Worlds. Every grave that was ever dug is here, somewhere, and every corpse returned to its final dwelling even if it had become dust aeons ago. We believe they are not conscious, but occasionally when visitors linger at a crossroads during the waning moments of the day, sighs may be heard followed by weeping.

They pass ziggurats constructed of stacked sarcophagi; there is no knowing how high these ascend. Catacombs belched from the bowels of the earth twist pathways into mazes, bewildering the senses, and obscuring the sky until all four have want of fresh air, water, and any direction that leads out; when they find it, they scramble and rush across bony terrain, cutting their palms and shins deeply.

At times, the Healers stumble across two gravediggers who stare at them unblinkingly until they move on. The sound of their shovels pushing into the dirt is more akin to dull knives piercing infected, purulent skin.

Their snickers seem to come from the ground.

Regardless of the direction taken, the Healers constantly return whence they came the time before. And when they attempt to plot their paths with a rudimentary map, the writing is unintelligible and when studied closely causes them to speak in a tongue not their own, and they rip the paper into frenzied scraps while crying bitterly and hugging one another.

All the dead are here interred. And there is no repose.

"Poor souls," a voice moans.

"Thou mayst rest," another croons.

"We have made a place for thee," another promises.

"Verily, loving crafted at thy births," the last proclaims.

At this, all four did turn about and seek the source of these chilling words. But not any living being could they see. Instead, at the base of their feet were four holes each sized to their exact measurements. If any were to take a single step beyond the path on which they quaked, that one would sink into their grave and be enfolded as though in swaddling perfectly-wrapped.

How fast and how noisily they fled. Their passions, though justified, were quite in error. For those things that slept roused, awoke, and were keenly aware of their fright and endless tears, and began loping after them with much sadistic glee.

"Such haste will be our undoing!" Hope cries out.

But how else could they respond to these threats? And so they run deeper into the convoluted architecture of this cursed abode for the departed, unknowingly dashing further and further away from all possible escape. They do not know that when they experienced the impossibility of perceiving their own graves, an inseverable connection was formed. There is something here by which causality is reversed, or coiled into knots as maddeningly disorienting as the slate pathways that lead everywhere except outside.

In time, this paradox will murder many innocents.

Lacking an unwavering connection to the divine, their abilities against the reawakened dead are paltry and not worth describing in full. Half-skeletal remains are stunned, then collapse temporarily in piles of bones before reforming; the most festering of corpses wail ear-piercing bellows that, when struck, crescendo above the range of human perception, causing themselves to explode into spewed gouts of rot.

The Healers are not prepared for such savagery as this. Each assault saps more of their willpower until they are stumbling, half-sensate.

"Daeli! Save us!" they cry.

Daeli does not hear them.

"Laurelai! Please, come back!" they beg.

Laurelai does not return.

Nowhere can they find succor, or relief, or pause to their torment. Whenever they enter an empty courtyard or landing or roof, another new horror worms out of a nearby window or doorway or crack in the wall. And at the close of the day, the very shadows cast by pillars and statues and monuments elongate nearly to the point of snapping, gain physical substance, and grab the Healers by the ankles and the wrists and the necks, throwing and thrashing and throttling.

Even nighttime offers no comfort while these shadows fade from sight. The glowing moon itself splits into shards, as though seen through a shattered mirror, and rains down dust that cuts their skin and burns with pain unending. It is this agony that causes them to notice the apparitions – or indeed, may very well have been the agent that caused the birth – of four vacant figures mirroring their actions.

None speak, nor have any fully distinguishable features, and yet the Healers know the names of these craven doppelgangers as if the memory has always been implanted in their minds, waiting to surface at the moment when they are weakest and without a chance of salvation.

For by our opposites do we know of what we value true.

Strife is bleeding, pierced by one hundred knives.
Despair is hanging, yanked snap-necked by a noose.
Avarice is starving, emptied through an inner void.
Hatred is boiling, scorched in skin-bubbling inferno.

And were the Healers warriors, a royal battle would here ensue. But these villains are not the unnatural and the unholy creatures as were those rejected things beneath Willow Way, rather they are the antithesis of the philosophies within each Healer's soul with which they have always grappled.

The living may die.

Ideas – in death – live on.

So, they flee as mortals may.

In flight they do find succor and relief and pause, though it is ephemeral and the torments follow ever after. Peace spies the edge of the graveyard, but the fence that surrounds it is another graveyard's beginning. Love finds a source of brightness that dispels their fears, but the lamplight blossoms that emit false dawn glow expel acidic fumes, then wither. Charity tricks blight spectres into attacking their pursuers, until each ghost dissipates into oblivion.

Then Hope held her ground, and here the turn begins. For she sought refuge in the past, where the others clutched frantically at a future that did not yet exist.

"That which was has ever been my guide!" she shouts.

And reaching into her bundle of curatives, Hope extracted the bandages soaked in the pools of holy water collecting in Kharhoom. Without thought or plan or hesitation, she hurled the wadded cloth at the highest point and smote it in its downwards fall with the upwards stroke of her staff. It burst in all directions a fog of holiness, flowing along the ground. Every droplet the Healers breathed filled their arms with courage and their minds with martial song and each beating of their hearts sang out a word that skywards once was sung from angelic throats:

Amen! Amen! Amen! Amen!

Now with senses fully returned, they use the lessons learned from travels afar to chart a course from calamity. They ignore the doppelgangers and the living dead, the traps of delusions birthed from fear and the doubts that pinion all action.

Instead, noting the tallest towering structures seen, they navigate by landmark and begin to spurn immediate sights. Where they are impeded by monstrous beings, they unite to break through, and continue on without delay. At times they separate from one another to solve bizarre puzzles that block their progress, but fueled by the power of holy water they call out to each other with stronger, bolder voices that carry across farther distances than would normally be possible, thus coordinating against encroaching dangers and slowly forging their escape. It is as they have ever done, but now with a revitalized sense of urgency for the deceased have begun to whisper into their ears.

"At first light, thou shalt remain," the whispers say.

"Whether divine inspiration, or a trick of this foul place meant to mock, I feel a permanence of truth weighing down those words," Peace declares. "If we are not beyond the borders of the cemetery, it is not the sun that will rise above that horizon of tombs, but something else, and something worse, and we will be trapped until the end of time."

Midnight rises from their four graves, reaching outwards like ravening and creaking jaws. The doppelgangers plod in their direction, undaunted, following the darkling tethers that connect the Healers to their fates. Weeds shudder at their passing; black dandelion seeds hurry to impregnate the murk. The Inverted Bell is tolling, each note reverberating the ground in earthquake: the footfall of an invisible giant.

A dark dawn is coming.

An endless night is yawning.

That which should not awaken stirs in sleep, opens one of countless eyes, and wonders upon the afterglow of dream.

The Wretched emerge from rough-hewn friezes that line the catacombs. The Wretched crawl out of defaced obelisks. The Wretched slink from the corners of their eyes, from out of the echoes of their footsteps, from the vapor of their panting breaths that condense like dewdrops upon the pitted sandstone walls.

Eyeless, they see. Earless, they hear.

And now the Healers must attack, for these ghasts are between them and freedom. It is a desperate struggle; every Wretched destroyed becomes two more, and those two four, until legion are their foes and Strife, Despair, Avarice, Hatred descend upon the melee and act as generals.

Armless, they strike. Voiceless, they scream.

Holy water is a boon, but their limited supplies rapidly dwindle. The remnants of miracle can only do so much. The graveyard's exit is not in sight; they cannot hear the silence they need to concentrate their magick; their staves feel muddy within their sweating grip; in their throats: words fail, prayers disintegrate, they choke on the dust of inevitability that is wafting from their graves.

The Bell tolls thrice. Matins is here!

Darkest Dawn!

The Sun! The Sun! The Dying Sun!

Love sacrifices his final drop of holy water, commits it to the Earth, nourishing nothing, and opens his mouth in praise of God, in memory of All Creation, with the full expectation to die in place of his companions.

And he sings. Such indescribable purity. It is impossible. He sings in words that are not of this world; he sings in verses that have not yet been written. It is impossible. The language of his aria does not exist; it may never exist even in imagination. It is impossible. Yet it is!

The steeple that houses the Inverted Bell materializes from invisibility, or perhaps it is crafted out of nothingness. And Charity and Hope and Peace are somehow singing too.

The fifth sorrow is healed.

Rejoice as I do.

There will be more.

This renewal is one that unites.

And so congregation begins:

Call
wayward
souls
home.
To the
bosom of
the lost:
tremulous sounds at night.
Lonely daydreamer with multiple faces,
lay down on warmed pillows of peace.
The fractures are mending upon the gilt glass
where the nightmares of nightmares now sleep.
Throw   open the windows in the morning   as wide
as the   world of my dreams had once   been,
and may   they too pass in the winds   everlast
with the memories   of threads and a pin.

The sun struggles over the edge of the cemetery, banishing cursed miseries away. Its light is dimming daily, but it is the same sun that has always been, consecrating the lowly dirt and that which sits upon it still. It creates shadows – but not ones to dread – of four weary travelers helping each other climb over the fence of the Graveyard of All Worlds.

One impossibility remains: the Inverted Bell is visible, enclosed by a new church that may or may not be real. None can say, as none have been able to re-enter the bounds of that fateful necropolis, to reach out and touch for substance, then return to tell the tale.

But every dawn and dusk, the Bell peals beautifully.

Apocalypse Relief

The Sixth Sorrow

Refugees throughout the world outnumber the dwellers of all remaining cities and townships combined. The last kingdoms have already fallen into destitution and chaos. It is questionable if civilization can be said to still exist at all. Farms are luxuries, rare, and dwindling. Those survivors yet living live off the land, and that is desolate indeed.

Floods of pollutants spill from Glassmere across the lowlands, killing off pastures in their wake, toxic embryonic fluid flowing between the spreading hills that open upon Cindercone Canyon. Effluviant liquid reaches the precipice and shoots outward for miles before falling to the craggy valleys below. The misty rainbows created are abominations of color: arsenic and rust, bile and tar.

The Healers discover hosts of evacuees huddled together on the rocky switchbacks leading to the floor of the canyon. In want of anything in their stomachs and with a desperate thirst, they drink of the waters raining down and grow sickly and weak. Charity distributes a drop of holy water to each one, and their sickness burns away and their vigor at once returns. But that will be seen anon to be a short-sighted kindness and a sacrifice stolen from the future.

Hope asks, "From where have you come?"

"Everywhere," answers the multitude.

And Love asks, "To where do you go?"

"Nowhere," answers the multitude.

There are too many people for the Healers to save. Briefly, they plead for a miracle. But the silence that responds to their entreaty muffles all sound until it is disturbed by the cough of a weary elder, the sigh of a stricken parent, the sob of an abandoned child.

They tarry, formulating plans, but they tarry overlong. At nightfall, a different kind of flooding pours from the cliffside above: an onslaught of the Wretched. Love, Peace, Charity, and Hope are not afraid; they bravely defend the retreat of the refugees, who flee downwards in panic.

It is a struggle seemingly without end, exactly akin to the vile spillings of Glassmere. Then the sound of a horn made of seashells booms from on high, a chorus cry harkens their hearts with words they have heard in rumors and song but never once aloud.

"In the name of the Lightbringer!" the voices exclaim.

And the Broken Crusade drives into the Wretched, pushing them off the edge of the canyon walls to their dissolution in the obscured and ashen depths of the ravine. While the Healers use this sudden shift in fortune to hurry after the frightened refugees, now fated to be their charges for good or for ill, they gaze back upon their saviors.

A single crusader, running rearguard, catches sight of them. She raises up the faded bleached banner, waving it back and forth in the morning light. For an instant, it feels as though the Harbingers are once more stalking across the horizon and this time Daeli will be victorious. The sensation speeds them onwards, chasing the defenseless masses down into the valley.

Peace be upon them always. For they cannot know that this nameless crusader – who did redeem herself, who did win back her name, who did live long enough to give birth to a strong and wise and good daughter – will die yet in glory, but nevermore be remembered except by this final phrase: she asked that her daughter be named her name, in order to pass on that which was sullied and cleansed by the same hands. I will honor the request for all eternity to keep her child safe, to remember she was the least of these that sought forgiveness, and with duty that forgiveness won.

And so the Broken Crusade flows up the choking river extruded by Glassmere, decimating the Wretched swarm until the noontide sun evaporates them and their corpses into dust. They will return, as they ever do, but for now the battle is over and humanity has earned respite until the sun begins to set again.

Down in the gorge the Healers seek signs of the refugees that, in their haste, did not know when to stop running. These men and women have lived in fear for so long that they know no other way. In time, the Healers spy them out beneath an overhang of limestone and comfort them with kindly words, embracing them fondly, and calling each "Brother" and "Sister" until they know their names.

With cleansing magicks, Love weaves a series of clever spells that filter contaminants from the stream that trickles by the improvised encampment his three companions erect. Though the tents the Healers have always used on their long journey – before the ending of the world and after – cannot hold many, the most infirm find shelter, warmth, and dreams blissfully empty.

And after an hour of helping, a rising echo of a miracle began to stir in their midst. Each Healer had been aiding each refugee with whatever need they had: washing away the ache in their feet; soothing away the pang in their stomachs; praying away the worry in their hearts. But when they had nothing left to do, they stayed awhile and waited to hear each refugee speak of the sadness in their souls which, for all of their prowess, the Healers could not fix. And then the children stood up from where they slept fitfully, as a flock of gentle smiles, and did as Peace and Love and Hope and Charity had – and more.

They listened with a wisdom beyond the years of time.

And then the whisper of the miracle blew further, softly, a fragile breeze moving them, tenderly, and every refugee began to go to every other refugee to ask: "What ails you?" and "How might I help?" And the Healers were much amazed to witness how a spark of an ember may kindle the glow of a hearth when compassion opens all hearts one to another. In the end, everyone sat together holding hands, and for the first time a gathering of humanity wept for the passing of the divine from our world.

"And yet," said Hope, with tears of joy.

Now secured and hidden from bone-warped scavengers and roving packs of abyss behemoths, the refugees ration their pitiful food supplies and prepare for a long wait. The Healers set out to explore the breadth of Cindercone Canyon for more survivors. Scouts travel with them a ways, foraging sufficiency of berries and honey combs and witchetty grubs, then turn back – after offering well wishes to the four – and hurry towards the encampment before eventide.

The canyon is a scar ripped across the land as though a mountainous blade punished the spine of the world with jagged, frenetic cuts until they cauterized from volcanic flow. The bottom of the ravine is steaming and the fumaroles reek with more insidious vapors than sulfur. Occasionally, otherworldly chants can be heard from those cavities along with the beat of a drum made of human skins.

"Are we foolish or bold to be here?" whispers Charity.

The chanting rises with an intensity that borders on the sexual and the violent and the perverse. Love and Hope look grim, and gripping their staves and grasping the hands of their companions hurry onwards and away.

Only Peace, after a deep consideration, speaks plainly: "We have asked of ourselves this question once before, and found our course to be true. Where else can we go but the hellish pits and the forsaken spaces? The innocent are not idling upon morning glory hillsides, nor the good tarrying within pools of sunshine, and the meek do not await us wherever they will. Nay, in all these places, I say to you they are lost. And what of the blind and the deaf and the dumb? How may we wait upon them and their dilemma, when they lack the means? We must go, I say! We must trek onwards though all the sins of the world would stop us! And what of Daeli? What of the Lightbringer? Is she, too, in grief among them? Does she not need us moreover? For my part, I will not despair. And if I despair, yet I will go on."

And thus Charity regains her resolve. And thus Hope and Love regain their verve. Peace has ever been the most quiet of the Healers, but when he speaks he speaks with a truth so clear that its profundity is a humbling thunderclap to the wicked and a comfort for the virtuous.

Between the brimstone-stained cliffs, the uneven ground is slick with patches of obsidian; some spray from Glassmere has somehow managed to reach this far, and turns each footfall into perilous hazard. Fortunately, the gifts of Laurelai again prove their worth and ensure the Healers stay upright and ready for sudden foes.

But their adversaries are here already and watch from up above along the face of the cliff: jaundiced eyes blinking, as broad as redwood trunks, with thousands of pupils squeezing into a single, solitary mass. Whenever the Healers pass on by without an upward glance, each eye rolls heavily skywards as if in anguished ecstasy. And then the ash, that dusts the defile through which they toil, lifts and begins to float behind them like miniscule birds of prey.

No sound is made by these dreadful motes that take flight, nor from the Healers themselves. It is horrible pity. For they think that they are careful, unseen and unheard, and ready for anything. And yet they are prepared for nothing, and are as dreamers asleep.

The ash forms into twisted nails and spears their bodies through. There is no time to scream or experience the agony. The nails then burst into powdery and blinding clouds, reform, and spear them through once more. The giant eyes above are shivering in passion, leaking alabaster paste that dribbles impotently down the rock face like excrement.

The canyon extends only forward; returning by ways known is impossible. Bleeding and hobbled from their perforations, they cast protective magicks – but these spells are paltry in comparison. This land is starving. It must feed. The pupils of the eyes are bubbling with lust.

Without a choice, coughing blood from punctured lungs, the Healers dash straight ahead into a bleak narrow. The nails are descending, readying their barbed spikes to pierce spines and skulls. Then, joining together in desperation, all four staves slam into the water. The ash avoids the deadly deluge by reversing direction, arcing high overhead where the canyon walls meet the bluffs, and begins to circle – a kettle of annoyed carrion-eaters.

Within this hallowed and most fleeting interlude, they anoint themselves with the last vestiges of holy water, bind their wounds with the final blessed bandages, and without delay plow onwards. There is no time. Daylight wanes, and the ash will surely fall upon them soon. Already the stream is soaking into the desiccated ground at the other end and will leave behind a dry bier atop which they will lie.

The reflection of the mottled colors of the sky in the water splashing around their feet causes them to remember their homelands. So distant. So far away in the east. A place of beauty they knew, upon setting out on their bold mission, that they would never see again. For that beauty had already sloughed away when they turned their backs, heading for this land where Daeli was said to arise.

But now a deeper gloom sets in four hearts beating in unison. It is comprised of the same word as before, but said with the acceptance of relinquishing their burdens.

They have come so far.

And they can go no farther alone.

So it is with sickening heartache when they behold the refugees appearing over the cliffsides, having recklessly slit their wrists and chests and necks to saturate the air with sacrificial blood, engulfing the ash and making it plummet. Releasing their most powerful spells, the Healers cry out. They are not thinking, they know not what they do, and their magicks mix with the ash and the dying men and women, and the emotions embedded in the ground.

The sixth sorrow is healed.

Rejoice as I do.
There will be more.
This renewal is one that wakens.
And so liberation begins:

Tableaus   of   intimacy   trapped
in   a   flashing   instant
so   many   images
transmuted to stone as smooth as regrets.
Only the memories are gritty and rough now
going to market counting supplies cooking meals
quarrelling and making love
dwelling on the yesteryear and latterday at once.
How petty. How droll.
How wonderful
to be a part of anything.
And then it ends.
Somewhere a lingering finger runs
downwards at an odd angle
as if along the ridges of my spine
and the Earth opens, and remembers again.

When the Harbingers had won, the triune volcanoes that give this land its name exploded. They extruded their molten guts with such monumental force and heat that the inhabitants here turned to glass, and ever since have lain hidden beneath the scoria.

None could have known what would be unleashed from powers commingled so haphazardly. But now those glass men and women and children melt, resolve into rainbow shadows of themselves, sanctify half of the refugees, then dissolve heavenwards. If God were not dead, It would receive them in the waiting place. But without God, they will wait eternally for a summons that will not come.

Apocalypse Relief

The Seventh Sorrow

A new ending dawns at the site of the first, but the sun will only rise one final time – as we remember it – unaltered. In this place, where an unnamed hill has collapsed inwards, the physical realm and the laws of reality cease to be. Grass and dirt and rock no longer exist within this boundary that grows ever wider, devours ever more of life and creation. And in its stead: one interconnected writhing mass of flesh, corded like colossal worms, creeping inch by inch away from the epicentre of Armageddon.

Our world has begun to digest itself.

At the core of this destruction is permanent nothingness. I cannot describe it any further. All failed attempts leave the impression that it is a blackness and a silence. This is untrue. It can be seen; it can be heard. But none of the senses can comprehend what is perceived. Or perhaps the anomaly tears from the mind of the observer all memory of the experience, removing any glimmering of what it truly is. I cannot say. And I also cannot say if that is blessing.

But what I can attest to are the concluding events and their aftermath; the triumphs and the tragedies; the names of the dead and the withered living. All, eventually, are one.

Laurelai is waiting. Her sojourn is nearly complete. Now armless, she raises her face to the growing daylight as much as her bowed and crippled back will allow. When the glow of morn passes the horizon, it soars beyond her sight. She strains to follow its fiery ascension with glistening emerald eyes, and when she can no longer: her tears are boundless.

Rapture!

She knows the time is now come! She knows what lies beyond it! She knows that she is not there! She knows the name of the one who is!

And in that endless euphoria, she awaits in patient zeal the peace and hope and charity and love that will usher her along the last steps. On misshapen legs and knocking knees, she is swaying. Jawless and faceless, she is humming.

This wordless melody is the same she once sang beneath the sun. And when all four Healers arrive and behold their broken companion, their tears evaporate almost as hurriedly. For the timbre and intensity of the notes are undiminished, and familiar, and remain Laurelai.

She commits an act of devotion by stepping from the pallid, barren ground onto a protrusion of pink flesh. Crimson blood pools in an outline of her sole, then dribbles in rivulets to the sands behind and starts to form more flesh.

Peace asks of her, "Was that step taken in accident?"

She shakes her head.

Hope asks of her, "Should we prevent your leaving?"

She shakes her head.

Charity asks, "May we go in your stead?"

She shakes her head.

Love asks, "Can we help you on your way?"

She nods.

And then the Healers of the Apocalypse said unto her: "Then we shall be your eyes when they cannot see. We shall be your ears when they cannot hear. When you can no longer walk, we will bear you up, carry you, take you to the hidden places you wish to be. From now until the end, we will be for you whatever it is that you lack. For, sweet Laurelai, you lack no hands while you have any of ours."

So the five went forth into the Land of Undying Flesh. They chose to believe in Laurelai, who could not share her belief with them nor would she have been able to convey in words the exquisite feelings that had first drawn her to this site, then back. They hovered around her, ensured that the path was certain even when it was covered in lakes of blood. They sprinkled water upon the leaves that had dried atop her head, silently cursing themselves for wasting their precious holy water on themselves. But if Laurelai had known of this remorse, and were she able to speak, she would have gently admonished them, and declined.

The way is arduous.

They fight off many-mouthed riven annelids that sup on the sinew underfoot yet hunger for organs more substantial. They hurry across shifting terrain that is rising as if drawing breath, that is sinking as if swallowing food. They ghost by the howling chortles of necrotic devilkin that claw from the wombs of blubber stippling the ground like warts, that couple with each other, that murder each other, that reseed the pulsing epithelium below with another nightmare pregnancy.

Deeper inside this repugnant land are distressing visions too numerous to detail, and the penning of which will benefit no one, and the forgetting of which is a gift to those who struggle still.

But the Healers are as good as their promise, and do not allow their eyes and ears and feet and hands to ever feel the burden. Some may come to think that this was due to their courage, or endurance, or resolve.

Nothing would be more inaccurate.

"What a blessing is this," Hope noted, "to be able to help a friend through this suffering. What a privilege to touch her, to reassure her that we are here."

That is when two marvels this world will never forget came to pass.

First, the Healers realized this feeling must have been what was the experience of God. And then the sun, now reaching its zenith, fractured. Tears of fire streaked across the heavens, so many colors both purifying and terrible to behold. The orb of light, that permanent fixture in the sky that instills wonder and transfixes all, suspended as though castoff pieces of an eggshell floating on spilled and runny innards.

But to Laurelai, who was by then connected to a rhizome infinitely larger than the forests of her childhood home, both events were the same and an indication that the true dawn was imminent.

For are not prophecies more than mere words? Is there not that pristine instant when they become real? And is that transformation not what we call history?

When all the mountains, forests, lakes, plains, deserts, hills, caves, glaciers, necropoli, and canyons are turned to dust, a song will continue to be sung somewhere, somehow, from someone's soul.

I cannot claim to know the nature of God, nor Its mind, not in the herebefore when It lived, nor in the hereafter of Its death. But I have come to believe from my travels, and my pains, and the things that I have witnessed, and the things that others have witnessed on my behalf, that regardless of the titles that have been given It – Mother-Father, Lord, Kyrie, Creator of All Creation, and the myriad of lesser names known only in the hearts of other mortal kin – that Its existence was a song that sang itself into existence.

We are the notes.

What we create of our lives, the melody.

By way of a symphony,

Concealed to all,

Laurelai has now become the sheet
On which a final song is composed.

... praise be that I have lived long enough to hear it.

And so the Healers, in awe of the celestial conflagration, take strange solace in the uninterrupted humming that emanates from Laurelai's throat. By and by, they begin to trudge again towards the heart of the unending mass of flesh. Skirting dangers. Resting for seconds. Whispering amongst themselves. Planning their steps, their route, their charge. Always taking care. Always watchful. They remember clearly the individual journeys that led them to each other, then led them here. They are so close. They will not give up.

At times, Laurelai stumbles despite their vigilance. But they are there to catch her. At other times, Laurelai is discomforted by the trapping of her body. But they are there to help her relieve herself. There is less and less of her with every step, and she scarcely resembles the faefolk in any way except determination.

And then it finally begins.
The promised moment.
The victory through suffering.
The ending of the first things.
The life blooming in death.
Genesis!

She feels it, propelling her forward, like the breeze of a hand on the small of her back urging her on. Another step: her greenery wilts. Another step: her skin dries like bark. She is weeping. Her sight is leaving, but there is an afterimage of sunburst glow in the very center of her waning vision. Her vision!

Daeli! **she cries.** I am here!

But Daeli is not here.

Daeli! **she sobs.** I have come as bidden!

But Daeli called her not.

Daeli! **she keens.** How I have longed to see your face! To be at your side! How I have yearned to feel your loving hand encircle me! Hold me close to your heart! Speak my name as only you can!

But Daeli knows her not, nor would she recognize her face or voice or name.

Daeli! **she begs.** Witness Laurelai as she witnessed thee!

But only the Healers are here to bear witness to Laurelai kneeling in supplication as her body, immobilized, roots into the ground. Her spine straightens unnaturally, and pale pink flowers sprout from the countless parts of her body which have sloughed away during her pilgrimage.

And the melody that pours from her elongated throat is lachrymose and absolute. Soon the Healers hold one another, overcome by the painfully sweet music after beholding their dear companion gesturing madly and gaping passionately at an illusion that only existed in her own mind.

Is that why the song of Laurelai is now so sad? Has her belief, too, deteriorated? Love and Peace and Charity and Hope speak as one: "We can not allow this." Taking hands, and encircling Laurelai – the dying fae who could have ruled the forests but chose instead to walk the Earth – they joined her song and gave it words.

The invulnerable, sacrilegious ire of the satanic creatures inhabiting the Land of Undying Flesh at once becomes aware of them. In droves they come, with limitless hungers and instinctual needs to rend human flesh until it joins the unconscious biomass. And the ground itself rises up against them: the Worm Tree burgeons out of nothingness, towering over, a visual blasphemy. Then its foulness further pollutes the air by excreting monsters of flesh from the fruits in its branches: the Flayed Ones, the skinless fiends that will one day become a more hated scourge than the loosed demons ever were in their prime. Whether with weapons or magick, this fight will not be won. So instead they empower, with immaterial gifts gained along the way, Laurelai's song.

"Preserve our faith, O God on High!"

Its passion clarified by righteous pains they endured.

"While goodness too on Earth is nigh!"

Its sustain reinforced by innumerable miles they trod.

"Protect our hearts, O Glorious Day!"

Its resolution ennobled by memories of those they saved.

"And let Your will divine prevail!"

As Laurelai died a mantle of blossoms draped her, opening in the direction of the vision she had seen. It was as if the brightest sunlight imaginable knelt before her, and smiled.

It is finished... Laurelai prayed, joyful in release.

The seventh sorrow is healed.

Rejoice as I do.
There will someday be more.
This renewal is one that creates.
And so revelation begins:

Nurture
and see
the rebirthing
prefiguration
this story who begins again those
that had yet to be and those beneath the soil that stir.
Raise from the hours of want the names of the valiant and
the names of witnesses   *divine. Glory is waking.*
Revise the promise.   *The word is reborn.*
Spirit, forged and reforged, remains.
Anything that was broken was meant
to mend, first its self and then its end.
Clarion call   *a single note*
affirming that   *choice to be:*
the resounding   *echo in my mind*
sublime   *identity.*

Every fiend petrifies. Beneath them, the pink and bloody ground dulls into chalky white. A groan pushes forth from the bowels of the Earth, and the rest is silence. Each Healer slumps in exhaustion, touching Laurelai and whispering her name. But wherever she is she cannot hear them, and kneels in the Atrium of the Second Dawn.

Even within great victories are staggering defeats. And some are permeated with a grief that follows further than the memory to which it is attached. Seven wonders have been erected around a land contorted by woe, signs of humanity's defiance against death and pestilence and famine and war. One day, it may well be enough. But today it is not.

And so, they do what they have always done – what all mortal kin alike have done from the starting of the world – and stand, brushing off the dust from their bodies, breathing deeply, looking around, and ensuring their companions are as alive as they.

Without a sun in the sky, their way will still be lighted but by different fires. Sometimes that will be of their staves, and others by only the lights they carry deep inside: those flickering, transient candles that must be cared for always.

The road will not be easy. But there are so many more that need to be helped. And if Daeli is not to come, then their stewardship must continue.

"Let us go therefore and wander everywhere."

Four separate souls walk towards four separate horizons one day to meet again upon the other side, with hymns of thanksgiving for those they saved in their ministrations. And a song carries from the lips of the Healers of the Apocalypse as they seek for you.

Bereave no more in the godsend age.

www.ingramcontent.com/pod-product-compliance
Lightning Source LLC
Chambersburg PA
CBHW071212130626
46555CB00004B/1684